To Mom, who graduated summa cum laude from Mom School.
—R.V.S.

For my Janelle, Laura, and Paul.
—P.B.

Text copyright © 2015 by Rebecca Van Slyke
Jacket art and interior illustrations copyright © 2015 by Priscilla Burris

All rights reserved. Published in the United States by Doubleday, an imprint of Random House Children's Books,
a division of Random House LLC, a Penguin Random House Company, New York.

Doubleday and the colophon are registered trademarks of Random House LLC.

Visit us on the Web! randomhouse.com/kids

Educators and librarians, for a variety of teaching tools, visit us at RHTeachersLibrarians.com

Library of Congress Cataloging-in-Publication Data
Van Slyke, Rebecca.
Mom School / by Rebecca Van Slyke ; illustrated by Priscilla Burris. — First edition.
pages cm.
Summary: A child imagines what lessons are taught at Mom School, which cover everything
from baiting a fishing hook to tucking you into bed.
ISBN 978-0-385-38892-4 (trade) — ISBN 978-0-385-38893-1 (lib. bdg.) — ISBN 978-0-385-38894-8 (ebook)
[1. Mothers—Fiction. 2. Schools—Fiction.] I. Burris, Priscilla, illustrator. II. Title.
PZ7.S3565Mom 2015 [E]—dc23 2014012962

The illustrations for this book were created with hand-drawn pencil line work, then painted with digital brushes.
Book design by Nicole de las Heras

MANUFACTURED IN MALAYSIA

10 9 8 7 6 5 4 3 2 1

First Edition

M♡M
SCHOOL

Rebecca Van Slyke

Illustrated by

Priscilla Burris

Doubleday Books for Young Readers

When I go to school,
I learn how to cut and glue paper,

count to 100,

and sing silly songs.

My mom says she
went to school, too.

I think she went to Mom School.

At Mom School, I think they learn how to go grocery shopping and not lose any kids,

how to
read stories,

and how to tuck you into bed at night.

At Mom School, they also learn how to
pitch a ball slowly so kids can hit it,

and how to go on scary rides at the fair.

Moms should never be late to Mom School because they might miss how to bait a fishing hook,

or how to pump up a bicycle tire.

At Mom School, they learn how to do more than one thing at a time, like talking on the phone and fixing my hair,

and making dinner while listening to a song I just made up.

grow ♥

Peppers

Mint.
smell me!

School Garden

Sometimes I wish my mom missed the day they taught about eating vegetables.

But I'm glad Mom was there when they taught about baking cupcakes

and how to build forts out of couch cushions.

My mom must have been the best student at Mom School.

My mom has a job she goes to every day.

But she says
her **favorite** job,

her **best** job,

her **most important** job

is the job she learned
at Mom School:

being my mom.